HAPPY BOY

NITIN JI

Copyright © Nitin Ji
All Rights Reserved.

This book has been published with all efforts taken to make the material error-free after the consent of the author. However, the author and the publisher do not assume and hereby disclaim any liability to any party for any loss, damage, or disruption caused by errors or omissions, whether such errors or omissions result from negligence, accident, or any other cause.

While every effort has been made to avoid any mistake or omission, this publication is being sold on the condition and understanding that neither the author nor the publishers or printers would be liable in any manner to any person by reason of any mistake or omission in this publication or for any action taken or omitted to be taken or advice rendered or accepted on the basis of this work. For any defect in printing or binding the publishers will be liable only to replace the defective copy by another copy of this work then available.

Contents

CHAPTER ONE

According

According to the International Monetary Fund (IMF), the Indian economy in 2020 was nominally worth $2.7 trillion; it is the sixth-largest economy by market exchange rates, and is around $8.9 trillion, the third-largest by purchasing power parity (PPP).[287] With its average annual GDP growth rate of 5.8% over the past two decades, and reaching 6.1% during 2011–2012,[288] India is one of the world's fastest-growing economies.[289] However, the country ranks 139th in the world in nominal GDP per capita and 118th in GDP per capita at PPP.[290] Until 1991, all Indian governments followed protectionist policies that were influenced by socialist economics. Widespread state intervention and regulation largely walled the economy off from the outside world. An acute balance of payments crisis in 1991 forced the nation to liberalise its economy;[291] since then it has moved slowly towards a free-market system[292][293] by emphasising both foreign trade and direct investment inflows.[294] India has been a member of WTO since 1 January 1995.[295]

The 522-million-worker Indian labour force is the world's second-largest, as of 2017.[276] The service sector makes up 55.6% of GDP, the industrial sector 26.3% and the agricultural sector 18.1%. India's foreign exchange remittances of US$87 billion in 2021, highest in the world, were contributed to its economy by 32 million Indians working in foreign countries.[296] Major agricultural products include: rice, wheat, oilseed, cotton, jute, tea, sugarcane, and potatoes.[249] Major industries include: textiles, telecommunications, chemicals, pharmaceuticals, biotechnology, food processing, steel, transport equipment, cement, mining, petroleum, machinery, and software.[249] In 2006, the share of external trade in India's GDP stood at 24%, up from 6% in 1985.[292] In 2008, India's share of world trade was 1.68%;[297] In 2011, India was the world's tenth-largest importer and the nineteenth-largest exporter.[298] Major exports include: petroleum products, textile goods, jewellery, software, engineering goods, chemicals, and manufactured leather goods.[249] Major imports include: crude oil, machinery, gems, fertiliser, and chemicals.[249] Between 2001 and 2011, the contribution of petrochemical and engineering goods to total exports grew from 14% to 42%.[299] India was the world's second largest textile exporter after China in the 2013 calendar year.[300]

Averaging an economic growth rate of 7.5% for several years prior to 2007,[292] India has more than doubled its hourly wage rates during the first decade of the 21st century.[301] Some 431 million Indians have left poverty since 1985; India's middle classes are projected to number around 580 million by 2030.[302] Though ranking 51st in global competitiveness, as of 2010, India ranks 17th in financial market sophistication, 24th in the banking sector, 44th in business sophistication, and 39th in innovation, ahead of several advanced economies.[303] With seven of the world's top 15 information technology outsourcing companies based in India, as of 2009, the country is viewed as the second-most favourable outsourcing destination after the United States.[304] India was ranked 48th in the Global Innovation Index in 2020, it has increased its ranking considerably since 2015, where it was 81st.[305][306][307][308] India's consumer market, the world's eleventh-largest, is expected to become fifth-largest by 2030.[302]

Driven by growth, India's nominal GDP per capita increased steadily from US$308 in 1991, when economic liberalisation began, to US$1,380 in 2010, to an estimated US$1,730 in 2016. It is expected to grow to US$2,313 by 2022.[19] However, it has remained lower than those of other Asian developing countries such as Indonesia, Malaysia, Philippines, Sri Lanka, and Thailand, and is expected to remain so in the near future.

A panorama of Bangalore, the centre of India's software development economy. In the 1980s, when the first multinational corporations began to set up centres in India, they chose Bangalore because of the large pool of skilled graduates in the area, in turn due to the many science and engineering colleges in the surrounding region.[309]

According to a 2011 PricewaterhouseCoopers (PwC) report, India's GDP at purchasing power parity could overtake that of the United States by 2045.[310] During the next four decades, Indian GDP is expected to grow at an annualised average of 8%, making it potentially the world's fastest-growing major economy until 2050.[310] The report highlights key growth factors: a young and rapidly growing working-age population; growth in the manufacturing sector because of rising education and engineering skill levels; and sustained growth of the consumer market driven by a rapidly growing middle-class.[310] The World Bank cautions that, for India to achieve its economic potential, it must continue to focus on public sector reform, transport infrastructure, agricultural and rural development, removal of labour regulations, education, energy security, and public health and nutrition.[311]

According to the Worldwide Cost of Living Report 2017 released by the Economist Intelligence Unit (EIU) which was created by comparing more than 400 individual prices across 160 products and services, four of the cheapest cities were in India: Bangalore (3rd), Mumbai (5th), Chennai (5th) and New Delhi (8th).[312]

Industries

A tea garden in Sikkim. India, the world's second largest-producer of tea, is a nation of one billion tea drinkers, who consume 70% of India's tea output.

India's telecommunication industry is the second-largest in the world with over 1.2 billion subscribers. It contributes 6.5% to India's GDP.[313] After the third quarter of 2017, India surpassed the US to become the second largest smartphone market in the world after China.[314]

The Indian automotive industry, the world's second-fastest growing, increased domestic sales by 26% during 2009–2010,[315] and exports by 36% during 2008–2009.[316] At the end of 2011, the Indian IT industry employed 2.8 million professionals, generated revenues close to US$100 billion equalling 7.5% of Indian GDP, and contributed 26% of India's merchandise exports.[317]

The pharmaceutical industry in India emerged as a global player. As of 2021, with 3000 pharmaceutical companies and 10,500 manufacturing units India is the world's third-largest pharmaceutical producer, largest producer of generic medicines and supply up to 50%—60% of global vaccines demand, these all contribute up to US$24.44 billions in exports and India's local pharmacutical market is estimated up to US$42 billion.[318][319] India is among the top 12 biotech destinations in the world.[320][321] The Indian biotech industry grew by 15.1% in 2012–2013, increasing its revenues from ?204.4 billion (Indian rupees) to ?235.24 billion (US$3.94 billion at June 2013 exchange rates).[322]

Energy

Main articles: Energy in India and Energy policy of India

India's capacity to generate electrical power is 300 gigawatts, of which 42 gigawatts is renewable.[323] The country's usage of coal is a major cause of greenhouse gas emissions by India but its renewable energy is competing strongly.[324] India emits about 7% of global greenhouse gas emissions. This equates to about 2.5 tons of carbon dioxide per person per year, which is half the world average.[325][326] Increasing access to electricity and clean cooking with liquefied petroleum gas have been priorities for energy in India.[327]

Socio-economic challenges

Health workers about to begin another day of immunisation against infectious diseases in 2006. Eight years later, and three years after India's last case of polio, the World Health Organization declared India to be polio-free.[328]

Despite economic growth during recent decades, India continues to face socio-economic challenges. In 2006, India contained the largest number of people living below the World Bank's international poverty line of US$1.25 per day.[329] The proportion decreased from 60% in 1981 to 42% in 2005.[330] Under the World Bank's later revised poverty line, it was 21% in 2011.[1][332] 30.7% of India's children under the age of five are underweight.[333] According to a Food and Agriculture Organization report in 2015, 15% of the population is undernourished.[334][335] The Mid-Day Meal Scheme attempts to lower these rates.[336]

According to a 2016 Walk Free Foundation report there were an estimated 18.3 million people in India, or 1.4% of the population, living in the forms of modern slavery, such as bonded labour, child labour, human trafficking, and forced begging, among others.[337][338][339] According to the 2011 census, there were 10.1 million child labourers in the country, a decline of 2.6 million from 12.6 million in 2001.[340]

Since 1991, economic inequality between India's states has consistently grown: the per-capita net state domestic product of the richest states in 2007 was 3.2 times that of the poorest.[341] Corruption in India is perceived to have decreased. According to the Corruption Perceptions Index, India ranked 78th out of 180 countries in 2018 with a score of 41 out of 100, an improvement from 85th in 2014.[342][343]

Demographics, languages, and religion

Main articles: Demographics of India, Languages of India, and Religion in India

See also: South Asian ethnic groups

India by language

The language families of South Asia

With 1,210,193,422 residents reported in the 2011 provisional census report,[344] India is the world's second-most populous country. Its population grew by 17.64% from 2001 to 2011,[345] compared to 21.54% growth in the previous decade (1991–2001).[345] The human sex ratio, according to the 2011 census, is 940 females per 1,000 males.[344] The median age was 28.7 as of 2020.[276] The first post-colonial census, conducted in 1951, counted 361 million people.[346] Medical advances made in the last 50 years as well as increased agricultural productivity brought about by the "Green Revolution" have caused India's population to grow rapidly.[347]

The average life expectancy in India is at 68 years—69.6 years for women, 67.3 years for men.[348] There are around 50 physicians per 100,000 Indians.[349] Migration from rural to urban areas has been an important dynamic in India's recent history. The number of people living in urban areas grew by 31.2% between 1991 and 2001.[350] Yet, in 2001, over 70% still lived in rural areas.[351][352] The level of urbanisation increased further from 27.81% in the 2001 Census to 31.16% in the 2011 Census. The slowing down of the overall population growth rate was due to the sharp decline in the growth rate in rural areas since 1991.[353] According to the 2011 census, there are 53 million-plus urban agglomerations in India; among them Mumbai, Delhi, Kolkata, Chennai, Bangalore, Hyderabad and Ahmedabad, in decreasing order by population.[354] The literacy rate in 2011 was 74.04%: 65.46% among females and 82.14% among males.[355] The rural-urban literacy gap, which was 21.2 percentage points in 2001, dropped to 16.1 percentage points in 2011. The improvement in the rural literacy rate is twice that of urban areas.[353] Kerala is the most literate state with 93.91% literacy; while Bihar the least with 63.82%.[355]

The interior of San Thome Basilica, Chennai, Tamil Nadu. Christianity is believed to have been introduced to India by the late 2nd century by Syriac-speaking Christians.

India is home to two major language families: Indo-Aryan (spoken by about 74% of the population) and Dravidian (spoken by 24% of the population). Other languages spoken in India come from the Austroasiatic and Sino-Tibetan language families. India has no national language.[356] Hindi, with the largest number of speakers, is the official language of the government.[357][358] English is used extensively in business and administration and has the status of a "subsidiary official language";[5] it is important in education, especially as a medium of higher education. Each state and union territory has one or more official languages, and the constitution recognises in particular 22 "scheduled languages".

The 2011 census reported the religion in India with the largest number of followers was Hinduism (79.80% of the population), followed by Islam (14.23%); the remaining were Christianity (2.30%), Sikhism (1.72%), Buddhism (0.70%), Jainism (0.36%) and others[m] (0.9%).[14] India has the third-largest Muslim population—the largest for a non-Muslim majority country.[359][360]

Culture

CHAPTER TWO

Visual art

Visual art

Main article: Indian art

South Asia has an ancient tradition of art, which has exchanged influences with the parts of Eurasia. Seals from the third millennium BCE Indus Valley Civilization of Pakistan and northern India have been found, usually carved with animals, but a few with human figures. The "Pashupati" seal, excavated in Mohenjo-daro, Pakistan, in 1928–29, is the best known.[365][366] After this there is a long period with virtually nothing surviving.[366][367] Almost all surviving ancient Indian art thereafter is in various forms of religious sculpture in durable materials, or coins. There was probably originally far more in wood, which is lost. In north India Mauryan art is the first imperial movement.[368][369][370] In the first millennium CE, Buddhist art spread with Indian religions to Central, East and South-East Asia, the last also greatly influenced by Hindu art.[371] Over the following centuries a distinctly Indian style of sculpting the human figure developed, with less interest in articulating precise anatomy than ancient Greek sculpture but showing smoothly-flowing forms expressing prana ("breath" or life-force).[372][373] This is often complicated by the need to give figures multiple arms or heads, or represent different genders on the left and right of figures, as with the Ardhanarishvara form of Shiva and Parvati.[374][375]

Most of the earliest large sculpture is Buddhist, either excavated from Buddhist stupas such as Sanchi, Sarnath and Amaravati,[376] or is rock-cut reliefs at sites such as Ajanta, Karla and Ellora. Hindu and Jain sites appear rather later.[377][378] In spite of this complex mixture of religious traditions, generally, the prevailing artistic style at any time and place has been shared by the major religious groups, and sculptors probably usually served all communities.[379] Gupta art, at its peak c. 300 CE – c. 500 CE, is often regarded as a classical period whose influence lingered for many centuries after; it saw a new dominance of Hindu sculpture, as at the Elephanta Caves.[380][381] Across the north, this became rather stiff and formulaic after c. 800 CE, though rich with finely carved detail in the surrounds of statues.[382] But in the South, under the Pallava and Chola dynasties, sculpture in both stone and bronze had a sustained period of great achievement; the large bronzes with Shiva as Nataraja have become an iconic symbol of India.[383][384]

Ancient painting has only survived at a few sites, of which the crowded scenes of court life in the Ajanta Caves are by far the most important, but it was evidently highly developed, and is mentioned as a courtly accomplishment in Gupta times.[385][386] Painted manuscripts of religious texts survive from Eastern India about the 10th century onwards, most of the earliest being Buddhist and later Jain. No doubt the style of these was used in larger paintings.[387] The Persian-derived Deccan painting, starting just before the Mughal miniature, between them give the first large body of secular painting, with an emphasis on portraits, and the recording of princely pleasures and wars.[388][389] The style spread to Hindu courts, especially among the Rajputs, and developed a variety of styles, with the smaller courts often the most innovative, with figures such as Nihâl Chand and Nainsukh.[390][391] As a market developed among European residents, it was supplied by Company painting by Indian artists with considerable Western influence.[392][393] In the 19th century, cheap Kalighat paintings of gods and everyday life, done on paper, were urban folk art from Calcutta, which later saw the Bengal School of Art, reflecting the art colleges founded by the British, the first movement in modern Indian painting.[394][395]

Bhutesvara Yakshis, Buddhist reliefs from Mathura, 2nd century CE

Gupta terracotta relief, Krishna Killing the Horse Demon Keshi, 5th century

Elephanta Caves, triple-bust (trimurti) of Shiva, 18 feet (5.5 m) tall, c. 550

Chola bronze of Shiva as Nataraja ("Lord of Dance"), Tamil Nadu, 10th or 11th century.

Jahangir Receives Prince Khurram at Ajmer on His Return from the Mewar Campaign, Balchand, c. 1635

Krishna Fluting to the Milkmaids, Kangra painting, 1775–1785

Architecture

Main article: Architecture of India

The Taj Mahal from accross the Yamuna river showing two outlying red sandstone buildings, a mosque on the right (west) and a jawab (response) thought to have been built for architectural balance.

Much of Indian architecture, including the Taj Mahal, other works of Mughal architecture, and South Indian architecture, blends ancient local traditions with imported styles.[396] Vernacular architecture is also regional in its flavours. Vastu shastra, literally "science of construction" or "architecture" and ascribed to Mamuni Mayan,[397] explores how the laws of nature affect human dwellings;[398] it employs precise geometry and directional alignments to reflect perceived cosmic constructs.[399] As applied in Hindu temple architecture, it is influenced by the Shilpa Shastras, a series of foundational texts whose basic mythological form is the Vastu-Purusha mandala, a square that embodied the "absolute".[400] The Taj Mahal, built in Agra between 1631 and 1648 by orders of Emperor Shah Jahan in memory of his wife, has been described in the UNESCO World Heritage List as "the jewel of Muslim art in India and one of the universally admired masterpieces of the world's heritage".[401] Indo-Saracenic Revival architecture, developed by the British in the late 19th century, drew on Indo-Islamic architecture.[402]

Literature

Main article: Indian literature

The earliest literature in India, composed between 1500 BCE and 1200 CE, was in the Sanskrit language.[403] Major works of Sanskrit literature include the Rigveda (c. 1500 BCE – c. 1200 BCE), the epics: Mahābhārata (c. 400 BCE – c. 400 CE) and the Ramayana (c. 300 BCE and later); Abhijñānaśākuntalam (The Recognition of Śakuntalā, and other dramas of Kālidāsa (c. 5th century CE) and Mahākāvya poetry.[404][405][406] In Tamil literature, the Sangam literature (c. 600 BCE – c. 300 BCE) consisting of

2,381 poems, composed by 473 poets, is the earliest work.[407][408][409][410] From the 14th to the 18th centuries, India's literary traditions went through a period of drastic change because of the emergence of devotional poets like Kabīr, Tulsīdās, and Guru Nānak. This period was characterised by a varied and wide spectrum of thought and expression; as a consequence, medieval Indian literary works differed significantly from classical traditions.[411] In the 19th century, Indian writers took a new interest in social questions and psychological descriptions. In the 20th century, Indian literature was influenced by the works of the Bengali poet, author and philosopher Rabindranath Tagore,[412] who was a recipient of the Nobel Prize in Literature.

Performing arts and media

Main articles: Music of India, Dance in India, Cinema of India, and Television in India

India's National Academy of Performance Arts has recognised eight Indian dance styles to be classical. One such is Kuchipudi shown here.

Indian music ranges over various traditions and regional styles. Classical music encompasses two genres and their various folk offshoots: the northern Hindustani and southern Carnatic schools.[413] Regionalised popular forms include filmi and folk music; the syncretic tradition of the bauls is a well-known form of the latter. Indian dance also features diverse folk and classical forms. Among the better-known folk dances are: the bhangra of Punjab, the bihu of Assam, the Jhumair and chhau of Jharkhand, Odisha and West Bengal, garba and dandiya of Gujarat, ghoomar of Rajasthan, and the lavani of Maharashtra. Eight dance forms, many with narrative forms and mythological elements, have been accorded classical dance status by India's National Academy of Music, Dance, and Drama. These are: bharatanatyam of the state of Tamil Nadu, kathak of Uttar Pradesh, kathakali and mohiniyattam of Kerala, kuchipudi of Andhra Pradesh, manipuri of Manipur, odissi of Odisha, and the sattriya of Assam.[414]

Theatre in India melds music, dance, and improvised or written dialogue.[415] Often based on Hindu mythology, but also borrowing from medieval romances or social and political events, Indian theatre includes: the bhavai of Gujarat, the jatra of West Bengal, the nautanki and ramlila of North India, tamasha of Maharashtra, burrakatha of Andhra Pradesh and Telangana, terukkuttu of Tamil Nadu, and the yakshagana of Karnataka.[416] India has a theatre training institute the National School of Drama (NSD) that is situated at New Delhi It is an autonomous organisation under the Ministry of Culture, Government of India.[417] The Indian film industry produces the world's most-watched cinema.[418] Established regional cinematic traditions exist in the Assamese, Bengali, Bhojpuri, Hindi, Kannada, Malayalam, Punjabi, Gujarati, Marathi, Odia, Tamil, and Telugu languages.[419] The Hindi language film industry (Bollywood) is the largest sector representing 43% of box office revenue, followed by the South Indian Telugu and Tamil film industries which represent 36% combined.[420]

Television broadcasting began in India in 1959 as a state-run medium of communication and expanded slowly for more than two decades.[421][422] The state monopoly on television broadcast ended in the 1990s. Since then, satellite channels have increasingly shaped the popular culture of Indian society.[423] Today, television is the most penetrative media in India; industry estimates indicate that as of 2012 there are over 554 million TV consumers, 462 million with satellite or cable connections compared to other forms of mass media such as the press (350 million), radio (156 million) or internet (37 million).[424]

Society

Main article: Culture of India

Muslims offer namaz at a mosque in Srinagar, Jammu and Kashmir.

Traditional Indian society is sometimes defined by social hierarchy. The Indian caste system embodies much of the social stratification and many of the social restrictions found on the Indian subcontinent. Social classes are defined by thousands of endogamous hereditary groups, often termed as jātis, or "castes".[425] India declared untouchability to be illegal[426] in 1947 and has since enacted other anti-discriminatory laws and social welfare initiatives.

Family values are important in the Indian tradition, and multi-generational patrilineal joint families have been the norm in India, though nuclear families are becoming common in urban areas.[427] An overwhelming majority of Indians, with their consent, have their marriages arranged by their parents or other family elders.[428] Marriage is thought to be for life,[428] and the divorce rate is extremely low,[429] with less than one in a thousand marriages ending in divorce.[430] Child marriages are common, especially in rural areas; many women wed before reaching 18, which is their legal marriageable age.[431] Female infanticide in India, and lately female foeticide, have created skewed gender ratios; the number of missing women in the country quadrupled from 15 million to 63 million in the 50-year period ending in 2014, faster than the population growth during the same period, and constituting 20 percent of India's female electorate.[432] Accord to an Indian government study, an additional 21 million girls are unwanted and do not receive adequate care.[433] Despite a government ban on sex-selective foeticide, the practice remains commonplace in India, the result of a preference for boys in a patriarchal society.[434] The payment of dowry, although illegal, remains widespread across class lines.[435] Deaths resulting from dowry, mostly from bride burning, are on the rise, despite stringent anti-dowry laws.[436]

Many Indian festivals are religious in origin. The best known include: Diwali, Ganesh Chaturthi, Thai Pongal, Holi, Durga Puja, Eid ul-Fitr, Bakr-Id, Christmas, and Vaisakhi.[437][438]

Education

Main articles: Education in India, Literacy in India, and History of education in the Indian subcontinent

Children awaiting school lunch in Rayka (also Raika), a village in rural Gujarat. The salutation Jai Bhim written on the blackboard honours the jurist, social reformer, and Dalit leader B. R. Ambedkar.

In the 2011 census, about 73% of the population was literate, with 81% for men and 65% for women. This compares to 1981 when the respective rates were 41%, 53% and 29%. In 1951 the rates were 18%, 27% and 9%. In 1921 the rates 7%, 12% and 2%. In 1891 they were 5%, 9% and 1%,[439][440] According to Latika Chaudhary, in 1911 there were under three primary schools for every ten villages. Statistically, more caste and religious diversity reduced private spending. Primary schools taught literacy, so local diversity limited its growth.[441]

The education system of India is the world's second-largest.[442] India has over 900 universities, 40,000 colleges[443] and 1.5 million schools.[444] In India's higher education system, a significant number of seats are reserved under affirmative action policies for the historically disadvantaged. In recent decades India's improved education system is often cited as one of the main contributors to its economic development.[445][446]

Clothing

Main article: Clothing in India

Women in sari at an adult literacy class in Tamil Nadu

A man in dhoti and wearing a woollen shawl, in Varanasi

From ancient times until the advent of the modern, the most widely worn traditional dress in India was draped.[447] For women it took the form of a sari, a single piece of cloth many yards long.[447] The sari was traditionally wrapped around the lower body and the shoulder.[447] In its modern form, it is combined with an underskirt, or Indian petticoat, and tucked in the waist band for more secure fastening. It is also commonly worn with an Indian blouse, or choli, which serves as the primary upper-body garment, the sari's end—passing over the shoulder—serving to cover the midriff and obscure the upper body's contours.[447] For men, a similar but shorter length of cloth, the dhoti, has served as a lower-body garment.[448]

Women (from left to right) in churidars and kameez (with back to the camera), jeans and sweater, and pink Shalwar kameez;

The use of stitched clothes became widespread after Muslim rule was established at first by the Delhi sultanate (ca 1300 CE) and then continued by the Mughal Empire (ca 1525 CE).[449] Among the garments introduced during this time and still commonly worn are: the shalwars and pyjamas, both styles of trousers, and the tunics kurta and kameez.[449] In southern India, the traditional draped garments were to see much longer continuous use.[449]

Shalwars are atypically wide at the waist but narrow to a cuffed bottom. They are held up by a drawstring, which causes them to become pleated around the waist.[450] The pants can be wide and baggy, or they can be cut quite narrow, on the bias, in which case they are called churidars. When they are ordinarily wide at the waist and their bottoms are hemmed but not cuffed, they are called pyjamas. The kameez is a long shirt or tunic,[451] its side seams left open below the waist-line.[452] The kurta is traditionally collarless and made of cotton or silk; it is worn plain or with embroidered decoration, such as chikan; and typically falls to either just above or just below the wearer's knees.[453]

In the last 50 years, fashions have changed a great deal in India. Increasingly, in urban northern India, the sari is no longer the apparel of everyday wear, though they remain popular on formal occasions.[454] The traditional shalwar kameez is rarely worn by younger urban women, who favour churidars or jeans.[454] In white-collar office settings, ubiquitous air conditioning allows men to wear sports jackets year-round.[454] For weddings and formal occasions, men in the middle- and upper classes often wear bandgala, or short Nehru jackets, with pants, with the groom and his groomsmen sporting sherwanis and churidars.[454] The dhoti, once the universal garment of Hindu males, the wearing of which in the homespun and handwoven khadi allowed Gandhi to bring Indian nationalism to the millions,[455] is seldom seen in the cities.[454]

Cuisine

Main article: Indian cuisine

South Indian vegetarian thali, or platter

Railway mutton curry from Odisha

The foundation of a typical Indian meal is a cereal cooked in a plain fashion and complemented with flavourful savoury dishes.[456] The cooked cereal could be steamed rice; chapati, a thin unleavened bread made from wheat flour, or occasionally cornmeal, and griddle-cooked dry;[457] the idli, a steamed breakfast cake, or dosa, a griddled pancake, both leavened and made from a batter of rice- and gram meal.[458] The savoury dishes might include lentils, pulses and vegetables commonly spiced with ginger and garlic, but also with a combination of spices that may include coriander, cumin, turmeric, cinnamon, cardamon and others as informed by culinary conventions.[456] They might also include poultry, fish, or meat dishes. In some instances, the ingredients might be mixed during the process of cooking.[459]

A platter, or thali, used for eating usually has a central place reserved for the cooked cereal, and peripheral ones for the flavourful accompaniments, which are often served in small bowls. The cereal and its accompaniments are eaten simultaneously rather than a piecemeal manner. This is accomplished by mixing—for example of rice and lentils—or folding, wrapping, scooping or dipping—such as chapati and cooked vegetables or lentils.[456]

Play media

A tandoor chef in the Turkman Gate, Old Delhi, makes Khameeri roti (a Muslim-influenced style of leavened bread).[460]

India has distinctive vegetarian cuisines, each a feature of the geographical and cultural histories of its adherents.[461] The appearance of ahimsa, or the avoidance of violence toward all forms of life in many religious orders early in Indian history, especially Upanishadic Hinduism, Buddhism and Jainism, is thought to have contributed to the predominance of vegetarianism among a large segment of India's Hindu population, especially in southern India, Gujarat, the Hindi-speaking belt of north-central India, as well as among Jains.[461] Although meat is eaten widely in India, the proportional consumption of meat in the overall diet is low.[462] Unlike China, which has increased its per capita meat consumption substantially in its years of increased economic growth, in India the strong dietary traditions have contributed to dairy, rather than meat, becoming the preferred form of animal protein consumption.[463]

The most significant import of cooking techniques into India during the last millennium occurred during the Mughal Empire. Dishes such as the pilaf,[464] developed in the Abbasid caliphate,[465] and cooking techniques such as the marinating of meat in yogurt, spread into northern India from regions to its northwest.[466] To the simple yogurt marinade of Persia, onions, garlic, almonds, and spices began to be added in India.[466] Rice was partially cooked and layered alternately with the sauteed meat, the pot sealed tightly, and slow cooked according to another Persian cooking technique, to produce what has today become the Indian biryani,[466] a feature of festive dining in many parts of India.[467] In the food served in Indian restaurants worldwide the diversity of Indian food has been partially concealed by the dominance of Punjabi cuisine. The popularity of tandoori chicken—cooked in the tandoor oven, which had traditionally been used for baking bread in the rural Punjab and the Delhi region, especially among

Muslims, but which is originally from Central Asia—dates to the 1950s, and was caused in large part by an entrepreneurial response among people from the Punjab who had been displaced by the 1947 partition of India.[461]

Sports and recreation

Main article: Sport in India

Girls play hopscotch in Jaora, Madhya Pradesh. Hopscotch has been commonly played by girls in rural India.[468]

Several traditional indigenous sports such as kabaddi, kho kho, pehlwani and gilli-danda, and also martial arts, such as Kalarippayattu and marma adi remain popular. Chess is commonly held to have originated in India as chaturaṅga;[469] There has been a rise in the number of Indian grandmasters.[470] Viswanathan Anand became the undisputed Chess World Champion in 2007 and held the status until 2013.[471] Parcheesi is derived from Pachisi another traditional Indian pastime, which in early modern times was played on a giant marble court by Mughal emperor Akbar the Great.[472]

Cricket is the most popular sport in India.[473] Major domestic competitions include the Indian Premier League, which is the most-watched cricket league in the world and ranks sixth among all sports leagues.[474] Other professional leagues include the pro football and the pro Kabaddi leagues.[475][476][477]

Indian cricketer Sachin Tendulkar about to score a record 14,000 runs in test cricket while playing against Australia in Bangalore, 2010.

India has won two ODI Cricket world cups, the 1983 edition and the 2011 edition and has eight field hockey gold medals in the summer olympics[478] The improved results garnered by the Indian Davis Cup team and other Indian tennis players in the early 2010s have made tennis increasingly popular in the country.[479] India has a comparatively strong presence in shooting sports, and has won several medals at the Olympics, the World Shooting Championships, and the Commonwealth Games.[480][481] Other sports in which Indians have succeeded internationally include badminton[482] (Saina Nehwal and P V Sindhu are two of the top-ranked female badminton players in the world), boxing,[483] and wrestling.[484] Football is popular in West Bengal, Goa, Tamil Nadu, Kerala, and the north-eastern states.[485]

India has hosted or co-hosted several international sporting events: the 1951 and 1982 Asian Games; the 1987, 1996, and 2011 Cricket World Cup tournaments; the 2003 Afro-Asian Games; the 2006 ICC Champions Trophy; the 2009 World Badminton Championships; the 2010 Hockey World Cup; the 2010 Commonwealth Games; and the 2017 FIFA U-17 World Cup. Major international sporting events held annually in India include the Maharashtra Open, the Mumbai Marathon, the Delhi Half Marathon, and the Indian Masters. The first Formula 1 Indian Grand Prix featured in late 2011 but has been discontinued from the F1 season calendar since 2014.[486] India has traditionally been the dominant country at the South Asian Games. An example of this dominance is the basketball competition where the Indian team won three out of four tournaments to date.[487]

See also

CHAPTER THREE

Australia, officially

Australia, officially the Commonwealth of Australia, is a sovereign country comprising the mainland of the Australian continent, the island of Tasmania, and numerous smaller islands.[13] With an area of 7,617,930 square kilometres (2,941,300 sq mi),[14] Australia is the largest country by area in Oceania and the world's sixth-largest country. Australia is the oldest,[15] flattest,[16] and driest inhabited continent,[17][18] with the least fertile soils.[19][20] It is a megadiverse country, and its size gives it a wide variety of landscapes and climates, with deserts in the centre, tropical rainforests in the north-east, and mountain ranges in the south-east.

Indigenous Australians have inhabited the continent for approximately 65,000 years.[21] The European maritime exploration of Australia commenced in the early 17th century with the arrival of Dutch explorers. In 1770, Australia's eastern half was claimed by Great Britain and initially settled through penal transportation to the colony of New South Wales from 26 January 1788, a date which became Australia's national day. The European population grew steadily in subsequent decades, and by the time of an 1850s gold rush, most of the continent had been explored by European settlers and an additional five self-governing crown colonies established. On 1 January 1901, the six colonies federated, forming the Commonwealth of Australia. Australia has since maintained a stable liberal democratic political system and wealthy market economy.

Politically, Australia is a federal parliamentary constitutional monarchy, comprising six states and ten territories. Australia's population of nearly 26 million[7] is highly urbanised and heavily concentrated on the eastern seaboard.[22] Canberra is the nation's capital, while the largest cities are Sydney, Melbourne, Brisbane, Perth, and Adelaide. Australia's demography has been shaped by centuries of immigration, with immigrants accounting for 30% of the country's population,[23] the highest proportion among major Western nations.[24] Australia's abundant natural resources and well-developed international trade relations are crucial to the country's economy, which generates its income from various sources including services, mining exports, banking, manufacturing, agriculture and international education.[25][26][27]

Australia is a highly developed country with a high-income economy; it has the world's thirteenth-largest economy, tenth-highest per capita income and eighth-highest Human Development Index.[28] Australia is a regional power, and has the world's thirteenth-highest military expenditure.[29] Australia ranks highly in quality of life, democracy, health, education, economic freedom, civil liberties, safety, and political rights,[30] with all its major cities faring exceptionally in global comparative livability surveys.[31] It is a member of international groupings including the United Nations, the G20, the OECD, the WTO, ANZUS, AUKUS, Five Eyes, the Quad, APEC, the Pacific Islands Forum, the Pacific Community

and the Commonwealth of Nations.
  Contents

www.ingramcontent.com/pod-product-compliance
Lightning Source LLC
Chambersburg PA
CBHW021815150726
47989CB00004B/1941